W9-BRV-580

DISCARD

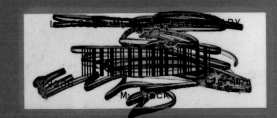

My Jack

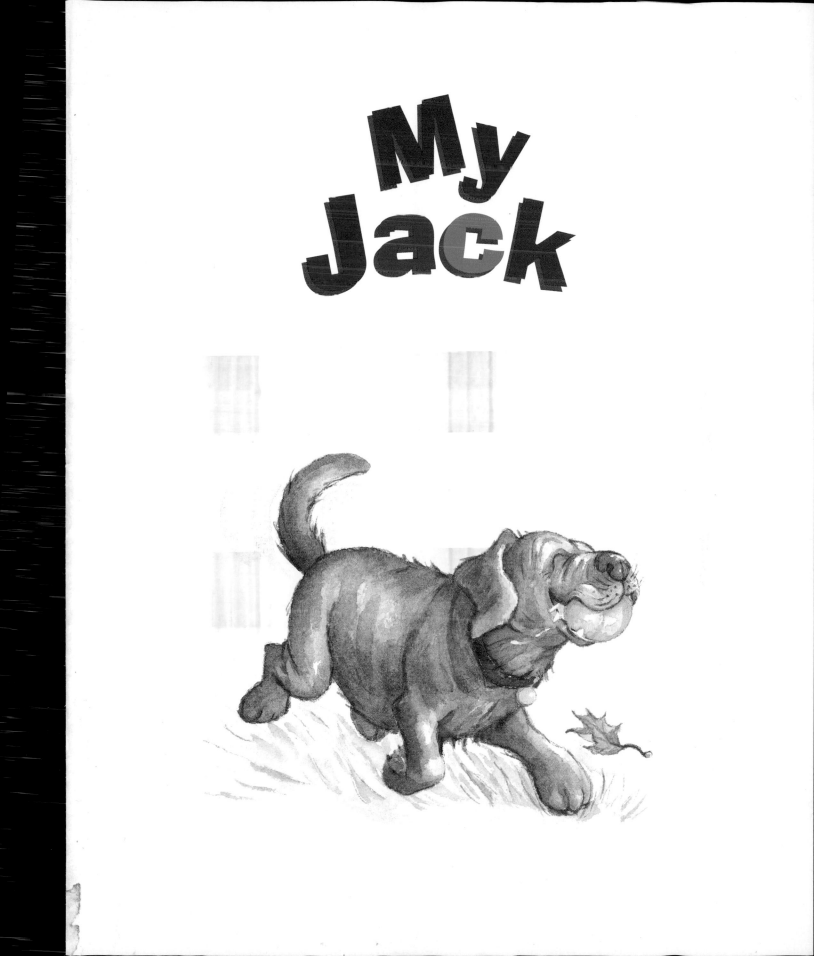

Whispering Coyote Press · Dallas

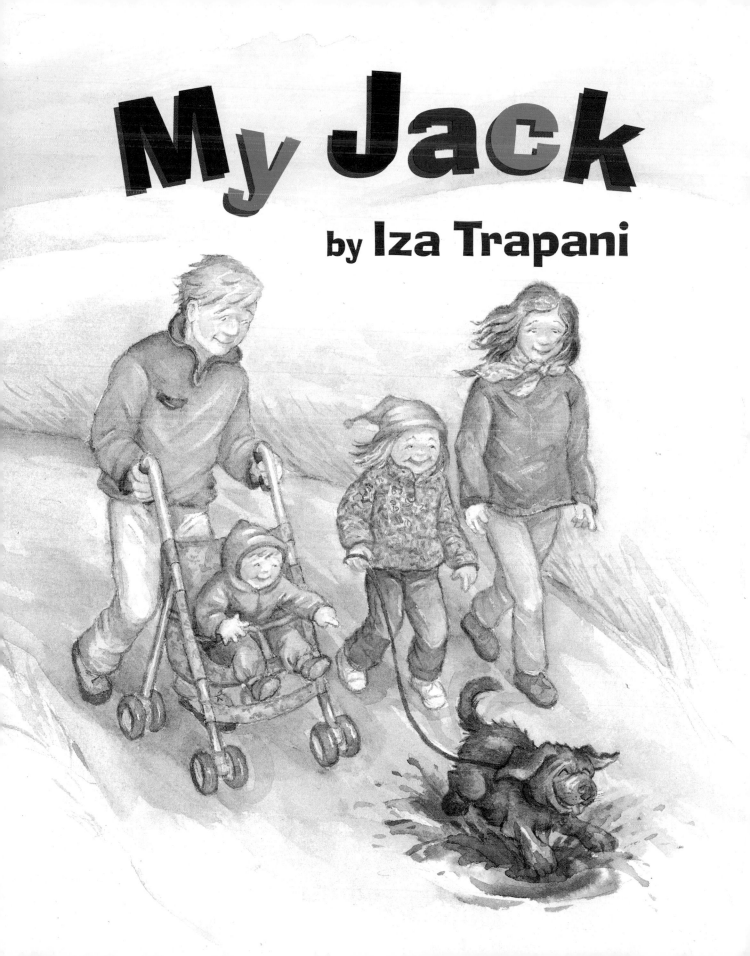

My Jack

by Iza Trapani

Published by Whispering Coyote Press
300 Crescent Court, Suite 860, Dallas, TX 75201

Copyright © 1999 by Iza Trapani
All rights reserved including the right of reproduction
in whole or in part in any form.

Text was set in 18-point Tiffany Medium.
Book production and design by *The Kids at Our House*
10 9 8 7 6 5 4 3 2 1
Printed in Hong Kong

Library of Congress Cataloging–in–Publication Data

Trapani, Iza.
My Jack / written and illustrated by Iza Trapani.
p.   cm.
Summary: A rhyming story about a fun-loving, loyal, and very
big dog and the child who loves it.
ISBN 1-58089-012-1 (hardcover), — ISBN 1-58089-013-X (pbk)
[1. Dogs—Fiction.   2. Stories in rhyme.]   I. Title.
PZ8.3.T686   My 1999
[E]—dc21   98-13229
                                                                  CIP
                                                                  AC

For Connie, who, along with Fuller, Ottley,
Mickey, Cobber, Little Brother, and C.D.,
can *live with the drool. With love—*
—I.T.

When Jackson was a little pup
I used to love to pick him up
and carry him the whole day through;
but then he grew and grew and grew

And grew and grew and grew and now
My friends mistake him for a cow.
"Just put a saddle on his back,"
Is what they say when they see Jack.

But he's my Jack, my big galoot,
So very goofy but so cute
And we're the best friends we can be
For I love him and he loves me.

My baby brother loves Jack too,
But he does things I'd never do
Like pinch his nose and pull his hair,
But good old Jackson doesn't care.

My parents think that Jack is cool
But they could live without the drool.
They'd like it if he'd clean his mess
And maybe eat a little less.

When all of us sit down to eat
Jack has a picnic at our feet
Then, as the crumbs begin to fall,
Our vacuum Jackson gets them all.

If friends come by to visit me,
Jack shows off all his tricks for free
And doesn't seem to mind at all
That someone makes him chase a ball.

No need for blankets on my bed.
I have my Jackson quilt instead
And now that I can stand the smell
My Jack and I sleep very well.

Then every morning when I rise
I feel his wet tongue on my eyes,
My ears, my nose, my chin, my cheeks—
And I don't have to wash for weeks.

My Jackson takes good care of me.
He loves to keep me company.
We draw and paint and play pretend.
I've never had a better friend.

He snuggles close and listens well
And keeps *most* secrets that I tell.
Well, yes, he did repeat a few
but I know *that's* not hard to do.

And, yes, he whacks things with his tail
And leaves a sloppy, muddy trail,
But, though he drools and makes a mess,
I cannot love him any less.

For he's my Jack, my big galoot,
so very goofy, but so cute.
We'll grow together happily
For I love him and he loves me.